William McDonald

Saved to the Uttermost

William McDonald

Saved to the Uttermost

ISBN/EAN: 9783337314477

Printed in Europe, USA, Canada, Australia, Japan

Cover: Foto ©Andreas Hilbeck / pixelio.de

More available books at **www.hansebooks.com**

Saved to the Uttermost.

By W. McDonald,

Author of "Scriptural Way of Holiness," "New Testament Standard of Piety," &c.

"Wherefore He is able also to save them TO THE UTTERMOST that come unto God by Him, seeing He ever liveth to make intercession for them."— HEB. vii. 25.

BOSTON:

McDONALD & GILL, Publishers,

Office of the Christian Witness,
36 BROMFIELD ST.

PREFACE.

WE have long felt the need of a small, cheap work, on the subject of Christian holiness, suitable to place in the hands of such as are earnestly seeking a better spiritual life — a work, unincumbered by multiplied human authorities, and unnecessary dogmatising, — which should, at the same time, clearly explain the doctrine, and properly direct the seeker to the attainment of the experience.

This we have sought to do in this little volume. We have guarded the doctrine against some of the more common errors into which many honest hearts, who are seeking light, are liable to fall, and pointed out the method by which souls may become established in this grace. We trust it may help some honest seeker to see more clearly the meaning of " an uttermost salvation," and to experience more satisfactorily that " the blood of Jesus Christ cleanseth from all unrighteousness."

W. McDonald.

June 10, 1885.

CONTENTS.

5

Saved to the Uttermost.

The inquiry coming from thousands of burdened hearts all through the Church, is not, What degree of piety is needed to insure acceptance with God, and membership in the household of faith? but, What is the believer's privilege under the reign of grace? To what extent have we the promise of being saved in this life? For an answer to such inquiries, we must consult the Holy Scriptures, and human experiences. If we are not warranted by the Word of God to look for entire deliverance from sin in this life, it would be absurd for any one to assume that he had experienced such deliverance. And if no such deliverance has ever been experienced by believers, though earnestly sought, a doubt might properly exist as to whether the Word of God had been correctly interpreted.

We are taught in the New Testament that we may be saved *completely.* Heb. vii. 25: " Wherefore, He is able also to save them to the uttermost, that come unto God by Him." The term " uttermost " in this Scripture signifies, *to the fartherest extent;* the *greatest degree;* the *most distant point.* It has been affirmed that the term " *uttermost* " has reference more to duration than to completeness; and that this view is sustained by the marginal reading, " *evermore.*" But the ablest expositors, as well as the New Version, repudiate the marginal reading as misleading.

Oleshausen says, " *eis to panteles* does not signify *evermore,* but completely, *i. e.,* perfectly."

Lange insists that it means, " completely, to the very consummation; *eis to panteles* is erroneously referred to time: the reference is not to His saving always, or forever, but to His saving completely those that come unto

Him. The perpetuity of His priesthood enables Him to carry through the salvation which He has commenced."

Dean Alford says: "Some take *eis to panteles* of time: He is able ever to save, or, He is able to save forever. But this is not the meaning of the word. *Bleek* has shown by very many instances, that completeness, not duration, is its idea; as indeed its etymology would lead us to expect."

Delitzsch has the following: "*Eis to panteles*, perfectly, completely, to the very end, but without, necessarily, any reference to time. Christ is able to save in every way, in all respects, unto the uttermost; so that every want and need, in all its breadth and depth, is utterly done away."

The New Version has expunged from the margin the word "*evermore*," and substituted "*completely*" in its place, which agrees with the views of the eminent commentators just quoted. In fact, there is no word which more fully expresses the completeness of salvation.

The Divine ability is pledged for a finished salvation — a completed work.

It would seem, then, that ample provision has been made for our complete salvation. The only thing needed to secure such a deliverance is to come to God by Christ.

Before attempting to define the doctrine. it may be well to guard the reader against several errors, over which many honest souls have stumbled.

In considering this subject we are inclined to go to one of two extremes — either place the standard too high, and by so doing, turn honest minds away from it as an impossible attainment; or place it too low, and thus inspire in ordinary believers no aspirations for its possession.

"If you would hit a mark," says Mr. Fletcher, "you must know where it is. Some people aim at Christian perfection; but, missing it for angelical perfection, they shoot above the mark, miss it, and then peevishly give up their hopes. Others place the mark as much too low; hence it is that you hear them profess to have attained Christian perfection, when they have not so much as attained the mental serenity of a philosopher, or the candor of a good-natured, conscientious heathen." — *Works*, vol. ii. p. 634.

1. *We place the mark too high when we make it to consist in perfection of conduct.*

Infallibility is not a fruit of grace. While human ideals of perfection leave no margin for innocent mistakes and unavoidable errors, Divine ideals allow many to exist in connection with perfect love. A perfectly faultless being, according to human judgment, was never found among men. No person has yet lived of whom serious complaint was not made by some one, not even " the man Christ Jesus." In Him was no sin. He was " holy, harmless, undefiled and separate from sinners." " In Him was no guile." This is the Divine estimate of the Man. But this is not the judgment formed and expressed with regard to His conduct by many among whom he lived, to whom He preached, and for whom He labored and died. They said, "He had a devil and was mad;" "that He cast out devils by the prince of devils;" He was a "wine-bibber," a Sabbath-breaker, disloyal to the government, and ought to die. Surely, if they called the "master of the house Beelzebub," we may expect that they will say some unhandsome things of His household.

Job is a case in point. God declared that Job was a "perfect man," and asked Satan if he had considered that fact. Judging from the conduct of Satan, it is fair to infer that he responded in the negative. He insists that Job serves God from selfish motives, and if the things with which Job had been hedged about were removed, he would cease to give evidence of that perfection which had been attributed to him. Permission was given to strip Job of every earthly good. When houses, flocks, herds, servants and children, were all destroyed, Job, surveying the utter desolation, exclaimed, "The Lord gave, and the Lord hath taketh away, blessed be the name of the Lord."

Satan returned to the attack, and insisted that though Job's earthly blessings were gone, his selfishness was manifest in his care of his person, and that should God touch his flesh he would curse him to His face. Satan was allowed to do his worst, without taking life. Job's sufferings were almost beyond human conception, and quite beyond human endurance. But in the midst of his deepest physical suffering and mental sorrow, without earthly comfort or human sympathy, with the face of God and man seemingly against him, he looks up confidently to God and says, "Though He slay me, yet will I trust in Him." Finally, Job's integrity is vindicated in the declaration, "In all this Job sinned not, nor charged God foolishly." But with this history before us, and God's declaration with regard to Job's character, it would not be difficult to find any number of people who are ready to declare that Job was not perfect —

very far from it; that he was full of imper-
fections. Our only answer is that Satan
affirmed the same thing, and God, who know-
eth the heart, denied it.

Human estimates of perfection differ, it
would seem, from the Divine. Men judge by
the outward appearance; God judgeth by the
heart. It is a matter of devout gratitude to our
heavenly Father that when He said to Abraham, "Walk before *Me* and be thou perfect,"
He did not say, "Walk before *the world* and
be thou perfect." Abraham could be perfect
after God's ideal, but not after man's. We
can be "perfect before *Him* in love," but not
perfect before the world in conduct. God
judges the act by the motive; but we are not
able to weigh the motive; consequently, our
judgment of the character of acts becomes
erroneous. We are not speaking of sins,
such as violations of the moral law; but of
errors in conduct, mistakes in judgment, etc.
To the human observer, these errors and mistakes may seem to indicate a wrong state of

heart; while God sees that they may spring from motives as pure as those found in the heart of an angel. We repeat, then, that a perfectly faultless life, in the judgment of men, may not be looked for in this world. So long as a difference of judgment exists among men with regard to given conduct, so long will a difference of opinion exist with regard to the motives which prompt to such conduct; and this ignorance of motives which underlie actions, must ever lead to erroneous judgment as to the moral character of actions. Hence we come to the conclusion, that to demand perfect conduct, according to human ideals, is to raise the standard of holiness too high. It may exist with a thousand mistakes and infirmities. It is "love made perfect," and not judgment made infallible.

2. *We place the mark too high when we make it to consist in absolute perfection.*

On no one point do opposers of entire sanctification manifest a greater want of candor, or intelligence, than on this. They have it that those who hold the doctrine of perfect love, or Christian perfection, believe, teach, and profess, absolute perfection. Such an idea forms no part of their creed, and never enters into their professions. They have ever insisted that absolute perfection is not only impossible to mortals, but that it can be possessed by no being in the universe except the infinite God. Not the holiest angel that lives and burns in the presence of God is absolutely perfect, much less mortals.

The perfection of which we speak, is a perfection which belongs to Christians; hence, called "Christian perfection." In quality it is as God's, for "as He is so are we in this world"; but in quantity it falls infinitely short of His. It is like God's, but not His. We repeat, perfection in quality is ours; perfection in quality and quantity, is His. So that we can be "perfect as our Father in heaven is perfect," and yet not be as God in perfection.

It is not unfrequently affirmed that there

is nothing perfect in this world — we need not look for perfection here. And yet we admit perfection in the kingdoms of nature and art, while we deny it in the kingdom of grace. We pronounce the flower perfect, the crystal perfect, the beast perfect; and no one thinks of calling in question the correctness of the affirmation. We say that the musician who renders the " Messiah " or the " Creation " correctly, does it to perfection; and an intelligent audience applauds the announcement. We pronounce the portrait which bears a strong resemblance to the original, a perfect likeness; and no one questions the statement.

Has God presented us perfect specimens of His workmanship everywhere in nature, and utterly failed to do it in the realm of grace, where it is to be supposed that He would likely exhibit His greatest skill and power? And is it true that man can do, perfectly, almost everything, except love God, and in this He is full of imperfection?

We pronounce objects perfect which serve

the end for which they were assigned. They may not be adapted to accomplish other ends; but if they do what their inventor intended they should do, they are in that sense perfect. It is no evidence that the machinery of a watch is not perfect, because it will not run a railroad train, nor that a locomotive is not perfect because it will not keep time. The locomotive was made to draw a train of cars, and a watch to keep time. If they do each the work they were intended to do, they are perfect.

It is no evidence that man may not be perfect in the sense in which God intended him to be, because he is not perfect in a sense in which God never intended. Man was not made to be an angel in this world, nor a God in the next; but simply to love God with all his heart. God made him for this. He possesses the perfection of saints on earth, which is "perfect love," or "love made perfect." This is the perfection possible in this life.

3. *We place the mark too high when we insist*

that it places its possessor beyond the possibility of being tempted.

That holy beings have been tempted, the Bible clearly affirms. How it was done, we must leave the reader to conjecture. Passing by "the angels who kept not their first estate," and our first parents, who were created "in the image of God," which consisted in "righteousness and true holiness," we come to our Lord Jesus Christ, who was "tempted in all points like as we are " (Heb. iv. 15); He even "suffered, being tempted" (Heb. ii. 18). If Jesus, who was "pure, undefiled, and separate from sinners"; who "knew no sin "; in fact, who was "without sin," could be tempted "in all points like as we are "; if He could "suffer, being tempted," then there is no inconsistency in affirming that we may be holy, and yet be tempted. It is not necessary that we have sin in the heart in order to be tempted, any more than that Jesus should have sin in His heart in order to be tempted. The world and Satan still remain to oppose, though the "old man," the "carnal mind," is destroyed.

4. *We place the mark too high when we insist that if attained, its possessor can never fall.*

The question has been often asked, "How can one fall, in whom is no sin?" We may not be able to answer the question satisfactorily, nevertheless the stern fact meets us, that such an event has transpired; holy beings have sinned and fallen; and what has been, may be again. Holy angels kept not their first estate, but were cast down to hell. Our first parents were holy, and yet they sinned and fell. Here are the facts which overturn all opposing theories.

Entire sanctification does not make men impeccable, as the theologians would say; that is, render them incapable of sinning. They are still exposed to all the dangers of human probation, free to stand, but at the same time liable to fall. To be saved from all sin will surely make it more certain that we shall not fall. To have all our foes on the outside is more safe than to have them both within and without. Salvation is by faith, from first to last, and he who stands at all must stand by faith.

Having considered, briefly, this aspect of the subject, let us examine the other extreme, in which it is placed too low. We are about as liable to fall into error in the one direction as in the other.

1. *We place the mark too low when we make it to consist simply in freedom from committing sin.*

It is thought that we can never be saved from committing sin; meaning, thereby, voluntary sins, — sins, known to be sins at the time they are committed. But surely this cannot be, for "he that committeth sin is of the devil"; and "he that is born of God sinneth not." "In this," viz., that one sins and the other does not, "the children of God are manifest," says St. John, "and the children of the devil." "This means *habitual* sinning,"

says one. No, it does not say habitual sinning; but simply, "committeth sin."

Freedom from committing sin belongs to
the justified believer. No man can retain his
justification and commit sin. Entire sanctification is far in advance of merely freedom
from the voluntary commission of sin. This
is too low a standard for entire sanctification.

2. *It is placed too low, again, when it is made
to consist simply in freedom from condemnation.*

A profession of freedom from condemnation is regarded by many, equivalent to a
profession of freedom from depravity; and
persons who make such a profession are regarded as wholly sanctified.

This is a low idea of heart purity, as freedom from condemnation belongs to the justified
state. "There is therefore now no condemnation," says St. Paul, "to them who are in
Christ Jesus."

No man is a Christian who is not "in Christ
Jesus"; and as none who are "in Christ

Jesus " are condemned, it follows, that freedom from condemnation is the normal state
of a child of God. As no man can be justified and condemned at the same time, and as
no man can be a Christian without being justified, it follows that every Christian must live
without condemnation, or he is condemned;
and being condemned, is not justified; and
not being justified, he is not a Christian at all,
because he is not "in Christ Jesus."

Condemnation comes of actual sin, or wil-
ful neglect of duty. Actual sins separate the
soul from God, so that no man can maintain
his justification who is not saved from the
commission of sin, and is consequently free
from condemnation.

Conversion is no inferior work. It is a
change so great as to be called a " new creation." If it is genuine, it will stop men from
committing sin, and free them from the con-
demning power of the law, and make them
obedient to all of God's commands. Do not
call this entire sanctification: it is far below
that exalted state.

Let us repeat, that we must not look too *high* on the one hand, nor too *low* on the other. If we aim at Christian holiness and miss it in directing our efforts to the attainment of the perfection of angels, we shall overshoot the mark, and very likely give up our hope and abandon the subject. If we place it too low, we may make a profession of entire sanctification, when, as Mr. Fletcher very justly says, " we have not so much as attained the mental serenity of a philosopher, or the candor of a good-natured, conscientious heathen."

We shall seek in the following chapter to describe the state of grace at which we are to aim, with the confident expectation of obtaining it.

CHAPTER II.

WHAT IS SCRIPTURAL HOLINESS?

THERE is an attainment of holiness for man in the body, variously described in the Scriptures as "heart purity," the "body of sin destroyed," "dead indeed unto sin," "sanctified wholly," "perfect love," "perfect holiness," "perfection," "loving God with all the heart," etc. What is the state of grace which these terms are employed to describe? What is it to be perfected in holiness?

It is to be cleansed from all *actual* sin and *original* depravity. Sin exists in the soul after two modes or forms, — actual and original, — the sins we have committed, and the depraved or sinful nature inherited, which was ours before we were conscious of sinning. This latter is called, "the body of sin," "our

old man," " the carnal mind," etc., while the
former is described as " transgression," " committing sin," " my iniquity," etc.

From the first — actual sin — comes our
guilt, and conscious condemnation. We are
guilty only for what we do — for what we
are personally responsible. Our personal
transgressions meet us like an armed man,
and our cry is, " Pardon my iniquity, for it is
great." "God be merciful to me a sinner."
God hears that cry, and takes away all *our*
sins, so that, " as far as the east is from the
west, so far God removes all our transgressions from us." This is the great work of
conversion, the new birth, or the new creation.
We are saved from all *our* transgressions.

The second form of sin, is called *original*.
It is that state which we call sinful, but it is
more properly depravity, or that perverseness
of our nature which comes of the fall. It was
in us before we were responsible for our acts.
This latter state cannot be reached by pardon,
for pardon can only extend to actual trans-

gressions, or what we are personally responsible for. We are not responsible for original depravity, for it was born with us, and is not removed at conversion. Let us illustrate the idea.

Mr. A. was converted — had a clear experience. He was full of joy.

> " Jesus all the day long,
> Was his joy and his song."

He felt no sin; therefore judged he had none. It did not stir; therefore he imagined it did not exist. He went on for weeks without a doubt, and without a cloud. He performed every duty, and was seeking only the Divine will. But in the midst of his duties and his joys, a man insulted him, and instantly a feeling of anger arose in his heart; for it is in the heart that anger has its seat. It did not come to the lips, for it was suppressed at once. But he felt the fire within, and wondered whence it came. He is humbled before God, and feels for the moment that possibly he has backslidden. But when he carefully examines the case, he is sure he has not backslidden, but has, to the best of his knowledge, been striving to do God's will. He does not feel condemned for the presence of anger, for it was not there at his bidding, and on its first appearance he sought to crush it, and did repress it. But whence came that feeling of anger? It belonged, no doubt, to that lower *stratum* of evil in his nature — that original depravity, which was not removed when his sins were all forgiven.

To get rid of this original depravity is the work of heart cleansing, of entire sanctification.

A pure heart, then, is one from which all sinful desires and tempers have been removed, such as pride, unbelief, envy, anger, impatience, and love of the world. These evils no longer exist to annoy the soul; they have been cleansed by the blood of the Lamb. Humility has taken the place of pride; faith has expelled unbelief; love quenches the fires of anger, and long-suffering puts an end to impatience. Hence a pure heart is one into which has come the unmixed graces of faith, humility, patience, resignation, meekness and charity.

So much as this would seem to be the radical, primary meaning of the term *pure*. "Entire separation from all heterogeneous, or extraneous matter; clear, free from mixture; as pure water, pure air, pure silver or gold." — *Webster.*

Its theological meaning, according to the same authority, is "freedom from moral defilement; without spot, not sullied or tarnished; incorrupt, undefiled by moral turpitude; holy."

The Greek term, *katharos*, means *clean, pure, clear;* and occurs in such texts as, "Blessed are the *pure* in heart." "Charity out of a *pure* heart." "Holding the mystery of faith in a *good* conscience." "Them that call on the Lord out of a *pure* heart." "*Pure* religion and undefiled." "Clothed in *pure* white linen." "The city was *pure* gold," etc.

This state is one in which the heart is simply freed from all that is impure — a clean heart. It is a heart from which has been removed everything which does not accord with the Divine will. A fully-saved heart can look up into the face of Jesus, and without mental reservation, say, " Thy will be done," while the whole nature responds, " Amen." This is entire holiness. There is nothing higher than this, when properly understood.

But this extends far beyond words and desires and forced consent. It means, " Thy will be done " at all times, on all occasions, and under all circumstances. It is, " Thy will be done " in want as well as plenty; in sickness as well as health; when the lights of our home go out, as when they shine with undimmed brightness. To be able to say, under every sorrow-stroke, as well as when surrounded by every earthly good, " Thy will be done," and say it from a full heart, and feel that our heavenly Father knows that our heart goes with our words, is evidence that sin is gone, the heart is pure, and Jesus has full control. But if depravity remains, it will rebel and refuse to yield. While we may be able to control it and keep it under, it complains that it is ill-used, and cannot submit. But to have

> " A heart in every thought renewed,
>   And full of love Divine;
> Perfect, and right, and pure, and good,
>   A copy, Lord, of Thine,"

is to be saved from all sin, and made perfect in love. A soul in possession of such a blessing can sing, —

> " Thou art the sea of love,
>   Where all my pleasures roll,
> The circle where my passions move,
>   And centre of my soul."

There is no longer a conflict between the inclinations and the judgment. The desires are no longer at war with the will. The seat of war has been mainly changed. Formerly we not only contended with outward foes — the world and Satan — but with inward enemies — our own unholy desires and tempers. Now the citadel is purged, the heart made pure, the enemies are without, and the fort royal is all friendly to the King. The warfare has not come to an end, but must be continued to the close of life; but our foes are all without.

Many and great are the blessings which come of this inward purity.

1. The question of our relation to God is settled. Until we are fully saved, such are the ups and downs with most Christians, that they have occasion often to inquire,

"Am I His, or am I not?"

The light, if it shines at all, shines dimly. While this is not the case with all, it is the case with the great majority.

But a pure heart puts an end to all doubt touching these questions. The assurance of sonship — that Christ is my Saviour, and that my name is written in heaven — becomes as clear as mid-day splendor.

2. The heart, being cleansed, is in a proper state to be filled with the Divine personalities. Before, there were obstructions. While sin did not reign, because under subjection, it still existed and prevented the indwelling of God, of Jesus, and of the Holy Ghost, in their fulness. But when sin was expelled, Jesus came in to abide forever. The Holy Spirit has unrestricted liberty to fill the soul with Himself. And then may we be "filled with all the fulness of God."

3. When the heart is pure, it is in the best possible state to enlarge and develop. Then, and not until then, is it capable of symmetrical growth. We do not say that the heart may not, and does not grow in a purely justified state; but it is a sad fact, that very few seem to make any perceptible progress, if, indeed, they do not decline. Their inward foes constantly cripple them, making it difficult for them to hold their own; while in a great ma-

jority of cases, they are overcome and fall into condemnation, if not into the very snare of the devil. When sin is cleansed from the heart, the only obstruction to growth is removed. It is like removing weeds from the soil from which you expect vegetables. They choke, they hinder, they dwarf every good thing around them. Exterminate them, and the vegetables have unobstructed growth, and a rich harvest may be expected. Remove sin from the heart and the growth of the Christian will become symmetrical and rapid, and he will become strong for labor and brave for the battles of the Lord.

Having described what holiness is, and some of its peculiar characteristics, we propose to consider the inquiry, How may it be obtained?

CHAPTER III.

HOW MAY WE OBTAIN HEART PURITY?

THIS is a difficult question to answer so that all minds may easily comprehend it.

We need to be assured of two or three things if we would be successful in our efforts in seeking heart purity.

1. That we are freely justified.

If we are not clear in our justification, we are more than likely to make a mistake in our experience in entire sanctification. If we commence in a backslidden state to seek a clean heart, and are blessed with pardon alone, and mistake that for complete cleansing, we shall find ourselves in great perplexity. We very much doubt if a person, in seeking restoration to the Divine favor, ever advances, at first, beyond the point from which he fell away. Such know nothing, experimentally, beyond that first attainment, and it is not to be presumed that their faith extends beyond their intelligence.

We have no doubt but that a soul, who has once known and lost the grace of perfect love, and with it justification, may, by the grace of God, regain the whole by one act of faith. They have been over the ground and know what there is to possess. Let every one, then, who seeks heart purity, be sure that they are already in the Divine favor — already know their sins forgiven. This is a good and proper starting-point for the land of perfect love.

2. Do not commence with the understanding that you must know everything about the subject before you trust God, through Christ, to purify your heart. There are many things you will not know, and cannot know, until you have the experience. If I were desirous of visiting some, to me, unknown land, — unknown, I mean, except from re-

ports of those who had been there, — it would be an unreasonable demand on my part to require perfect information with regard to all the various appearances of the way, and all the possible contingencies of the journey, before I would consent to set out. It would be quite enough, says one, for me to have satisfactory evidence that the land was accessible, that the way was feasible, and that the proper exercise of my natural powers of body and mind would bring me there. If I were wise, with these evidences before me, I should no longer speculate upon matters which I could never fully understand until they came under my own personal observation.

3. Be sure you do not seek another's experience. Many persons are liable to fall into this error. They have heard some wonderful experience related. It has the elements of the marvelous in it. There was the "rushing wind," the "tongue of fire," the angelic rapture, the prostration of the body, the third-heaven vision, either in the body or out of

the body. Or, there may have been the
absence of these ecstasies, and the "still
small voice," the speechless awe," the "soul-
rest," the hush of peace, the "heaven of
love." But if you would be successful, seek
none of these. Do not seek any particular
experience, for, generally, what you seek is
not what God sees is best for you. Seek
Christ, the Cleanser. He will give you such
an experience as will be suited to your temperament, and to the work to which He calls
you.

4. Do not make the mistake, in seeking
heart purity, of seeking it from selfish
motives.

This may seem an unnecessary warning.
But we are liable to fail at this point. We
are not useful, we are not happy, we are not
successful in Christian work. We see others
more useful, more successful, more happy,
and we are impressed that it is because they
are more holy. If we were more holy, we,
too, would be able to pray with more free-

dom, speak with greater power, and draw around us a more enthusiastic crowd. We would be more popular, more sought after, more influential, more useful. There may be more or less of selfishness mixed with all of this. There is one reason assigned by God why we should be holy, — not that we may be happy, or useful, or popular, — but, "Be ye holy, for I am holy." We are to be holy that we may be like our Father, and our elder Brother. We are to be holy because God has commanded it, and because it is right that we should be holy. We should be holy if we are not happy, if we are not popular, if we are not useful, — provided God has commanded it. He can get along with this world if we are neither popular nor useful in it; and as for happiness, we can better afford to be without it here than to be without heaven hereafter. We do not mean to insinuate that happiness and usefulness do not come of holiness, but they should not be the motives which prompt us to seek it.

5. No great progress is made in seeking en
tire sanctification, until it becomes the all-ab
sorbing subject of the soul's longings. There
must be a deep conviction for holiness; a
loathing of the evils of the heart, and a cry
for God which will not be denied. Such conviction does not necessarily imply *condemnation*, but *soul-need*. Condemnation comes of
actual transgression, while conviction for holiness comes of felt depravity. Until we desire
purity of heart more than we desire any earthly good; until we are willing to make any
sacrifice to obtain it; until we are willing to
actually part with life itself rather than not
secure it, it will elude our grasp.

It often occurs that such soul-appalling
views of one's impurity are presented, that
the soul almost gives up in despair, and con-
cludes they were never converted, or if ever
converted, they have lost the blessing. Such
views should not discourage us. God is show-
ing us our heart as we have not seen it before, that we may press our way to the foun-
tain of cleansing.

If we would succeed in seeking heart purity, we must —

I. *See that our consecration is complete.*

By consecration we mean an unreserved devotement of ourselves to God, bringing body, soul, talents, possessions, reputation — all our " being's ransomed powers " — to God.

It is claimed that we do all this at conversion, and have no need to repeat it. They who say this know little of what consecration means. But as we do not wish to divert the reader's attention from the one important point, by controversy, we will simply state what all must confess to be true.

1. When we came to God for pardon we had no intelligent idea of what was meant by consecration, if, indeed, we had ever heard the word in such connection. Now, we know its import, and are able, to some extent, to see the propriety of the duty.

2. When we came to God for pardon, we were dead in trespasses and sins, and must, of necessity, bring dead powers. Indeed, we

were *felons*, and had nothing to consecrate. We were under sentence of death, awaiting execution. Free pardon or endless doom was all we could expect. Talk of a felon making his will, and consecrating himself and his effects to the government! Bishop Taylor relates the case of a man tried and convicted of murder, and sentenced to be executed. Every effort which social influence and wealth could make for his pardon, or the commutation of his sentence, was made; but all in vain. When the fact was finally made known to the wretched man that he must die, he said to his counsel: "Bring me some stationery: I want to make my will." His friend said to him : "Doctor, if you will consider a moment, you will see that you have no power to make a will. In the eyes of the law you are as much a dead man as you will be after your execution." The doomed man saw the point, and turned away and wept. This is our condition on our approach to Christ for pardon. We are doomed to death — "con-

demned already." Our only hope is in a free
pardon, which is mercifully granted through
Jesus Christ our Lord, on condition that we
make an unconditional surrender as a doomed
felon. But now, having been "made alive
from the dead," we are able to bring ourselves
a "living sacrifice," "which is our reasonable
service." We are citizens, now, and our civil
rights are restored to us; consequently we
have something to bring.

3. When we came to God for pardon, we had
no idea of "hands" and "feet" and "voice"
and "will" and "heart" and "moments" and
"silver" and "gold" and "all," to be used
when, as, and to the extent heaven required.
We just massed our offering, and said, —

> "Here, Lord, I give myself away,
> 'Tis all that I can do."

Now we come, intelligently praying, —

> "Take my soul and body's powers,
> Take my memory, mind, and will,
> All my goods and all my hours,
> All I know and all I feel,

. All I think, or speak, or do —
Take my heart, and make it new."

The difficulty in our consecration will turn on some single point. It is very likely to centre around some forbidden indulgence, or some specially difficult duty. Satan will turn us from the path at this point if possible. He will magnify a mole-hill into a mountain, and persuade us to believe that we can never succeed. He may tempt us to believe that if we are entirely sanctified, God will impose upon us duties which we shall not be able to perform, or demand of us acts which will render us odious in the eyes of intelligent people.

It is not to be supposed that God will require anything which He will not give us power to perform. God is not accustomed to require impossibilities of His people. We may be assured that whatever God demands, He will see that we are able to perform.

Then, God has as much respect for what is proper, as we have. He would not be likely to require of us any outlandish acts, such as would prejudice His cause; and any acts which He approves, and which will promote the interests of holiness, should be cheerfully performed by us.

This unwillingness to submit to God and allow Him to " direct our paths," is the clearest evidence that we do not fully devote ourselves to Him. There is no more beautiful description of entire consecration than that found in Miss Frances Ridley Havergal's hymn. Let us consider it in detail : —

> " Take my life and let it be
> Consecrated, Lord, to Thee."

This includes the whole being. Then follow the particulars in which we are to be consecrated : —

> " Take my hands and let them move
> At the impulse of Thy love."

These hands are to be consecrated to God, so that they shall perform His bidding. Whatever our hands do, must be done for Jesus — all our earthly labor. Business is to be done,

not as the world does it, but as God requires
—"at the impulse of Thy love."

> "Take my feet and let them be
> Swift and beautiful for Thee."

Our steps are not only to be ordered of the
Lord, but we are to heed that ordering. If
we take a journey — go to this or that place
— we must see to it that our steps are ordered
of the Lord. If we are tempted to go to the
house of pleasure or amusement, we are to remember that our feet are consecrated to God,
and are to run only in the ways of His com-
mandments.

> "Take my voice and let me sing
> Always, only, for my King."

If we have been accustomed to sing those
songs which do not tend "to the knowledge
and love of God," they must be abandoned
for Jesus, and our singing mnst be for Him.
And this is not to be done for a brief season,
but "always"; not a part for the one and a
part for the other, but "only for our King."

"Take my lips and let them be
Filled with messages from Thee."

If we have used our lips in speaking evil of others, or for vain and foolish conversation, that must be abandoned now and forever, and only words of charity fall from your lips. If we have indulged in light story-telling, — stories of a questionable morality, — all this must come to an end. If we have failed to testify for Jesus, from this time to the end of life we must be a humble witness for Him.

"Take my moments and my days,
Let them flow in ceaseless praise."

Our time is not our own. Every moment is the Lord's, and must be devoted to Him. There is no time to squander, no time to spend in useless pursuits, no time for mere pleasure. Our moments are all the Lord's, and must be consecrated to Him. How much time we have misspent! now lost, and lost forever! The little remaining is to be fully the Lord's.

"Take my will and make it Thine:
It shall be no longer mine."

We are to have no will of our own. By this is meant, that our will is to be in perfect subjection to the Divine will — that we are to have no will opposed to His. Our will is to give way at all times, and His is to be recognized as superior. If our wills are consecrated, all else goes without effort.

> "Take my heart — it is Thine own:
> It shall be Thy royal throne."

My heart is to be kept as the presence-chamber of the King. He only has a right to its occupancy; and if another is to be admitted, it must be by His permission, and it must not be another that will cause us to divide our affections.

> "Take my love, — my Lord, I pour
> At Thy feet its treasure-store."

We are to consecrate our affections to Him — to Him only. If we love others, it must be for His sake, and for His glory.

> "Take myself, and I will be
> Ever, only, all for Thee!"

It is finally all included in "myself," — my whole being — all I have, all I am, all I can or may do — *all* for Thee, *ever* for Thee, *only* for Thee.

This is consecration. It has a wider range when taken in detail, but it is all summed up in " my *will*," " *myself.*"

If we are not fully consecrated, we must resolve that this work shall be done at once. Ask God to show us what we do not see. Let us lay our hearts open to His inspection, and be willing that He should see all, and know all. The Spirit of God is ever ready to help us. He will shine on our darkness, and discover all the hidden evils of the soul. At every cost, let Him have all — let Him have it now — let Him have it forever. We need not be deceived — God will not disappoint us, but will give us the desire of our hearts. If we have reached the point where we are will-ing to *be* whatever God requires, and *do* whatever He commands, and *suffer* whatever His providence may appoint, we are where we may trust that the work is done. Not that it is done because we have consecrated all to God, but, having consecrated all, we may believe that God does what He has promised to do, "save us to the uttermost."

II. *What are we to believe in order to be fully sanctified?*

We are to believe, —

1. That God is *able* to save us from all our sins: that there is no want of ability on His part. Do we believe this, or have we lingering doubts on the subject? Doubt no more.

2. We are to believe that God is not only *able*, but *willing* to save us. We may believe He is *able*, but doubt His *willingness* to save us fully, The smallest doubt here bars the Spirit's work, and leaves us without a pure heart. He must be *willing*, for He hates sin with perfect hatred, and would rejoice to free His people from moral pollution.

3. We must believe that God is not only *able* and *willing*, but ready to do it *now*. As "*now* is the day of salvation," there can be

no salvation for any time but *now*. We shall find it difficult to bring our hearts to say, *now*. We are so much inclined to place it in the future! — any time but *now*.

4. To all this must be added a trust or belief that He *doeth* it — doeth it *when* we pray — *when* we ask.

Take the following promises upon which to rest our faith: " Him that cometh unto me I will in no wise cast out." We come unto Jesus, and this promise covers our case. " If ye shall ask anything in My name, I will do it." This means, if we ask anything which God has promised. Has He promised heart purity? Let Him answer: " If we confess our sins, He is faithful and just to forgive us our sins, and to cleanse us from all unrighteousness." But may I ask and receive it now? Here is the answer: " What things soever ye desire when ye pray, believe that ye *receive* them, and ye shall have them. Here we are required to believe that we *receive*, when we pray, in order that we may have.

But how can we believe that we *have*, before we have? We cannot; nor are we required thus to do. God does not say, Believe that you *have;* but believe that you *receive*, and you SHALL have. God holds out the gift and says, Take it, and make it yours. We reach out our hand to receive what is offered. And as we reach out the hand, or trust, He bestows, and then we *have* what our faith claims. It requires no great effort, and yet it is not clear to the unsaved soul. We think we must struggle and make a great effort. But we shall find in the end that little good comes of all " bodily exercise." Faith is so simple, so nearly nothing, that we overlook its true character. It is not carrying away, Samson-like, the gates of Gaza, but it is simply leaning over, in our great weakness, upon the loving heart of the world's Redeemer, and feeling that all our strength is in Him. And yet we are not to cease our cry for freedom till freedom comes.

A brother, earnestly seeking heart purity,

and confessing he was so blind he did not know how to believe, asked, " What do we do when we believe?" He was told that believing was "simply saying *Amen*, to God "; and as he said it, freedom came to his soul, and he rejoiced in the possession of that grace he so long and so ardently sought. Many have found this great blessing. They are in all branches of the Christian Church. They all tell about the same story. It is with them all, simple consecration, or devotement, and trust. Then the new life of freedom is enjoyed.

This second experience differs from the first in several particulars; we notice only two.

1. In conversion, our sins are pardoned and we are fully justified, and become members of the household of faith, with a title to our everlasting inheritance. In entire sanctification, we are cleansed from all impurity, and are made meet for the kingdom of glory.

2. In conversion, the soul rests from fear,

and no longer feels condemnation for its past sins. In entire sanctification, the war within, creating discordances, has come to an end. The carnal mind has been removed, the old man cast out, and the reign of grace is complete. The troubled one has found

"A rest where all our soul's desire
Is fixed on things above;
Where fear, and sin, and grief expire,
Cast out by perfect love."

The experience is variously described. Mr. Bramwell says: "My soul was all wonder, love, and praise." Mrs. Hester Ann Rogers says: "I am conquered and subdued by love. . . . Sin — inbred sin — no longer hinders the close communion, and God is all my own." Dr. T. C. Upham says: "There was no intellectual excitement, no very marked joy, when I reached this great rock of practical salvation. But I was distinctly conscious when I reached it." James Brainerd Taylor says: "All was calm and tranquil, silent and solemn, and a heaven of love pervaded my whole soul." Bishop Whatcoat says: "Suddenly I was stripped of all but love." Bishop Hamline says: "I felt it not only outwardly, but inwardly. It seemed to press upon my whole being, and to diffuse all through and through it, a holy, sin-consuming energy. For a few minutes, the deep of God's love swallowed me up, — all its waves and billows rolled over me."

Let us not be betrayed into seeking any or all of these experiences, *as experiences.* Seek *Him,* the *Sanctifier,* and "with Himself He will freely give us all things."

Be certain that your consecration is complete. If a matter arises, of the propriety of which you are uncertain, let it go. Give God the benefit of the doubt. Let Him have all, and have it for all time. You need not be deceived here, for if there be anything lacking, "God will reveal even this unto you." Come honestly, and God will make it plain.

When you have given all, then "rest upon

His promise sure." Never depart. He cannot deny Himself. You shall know that the work is done.

CHAPTER IV.

HOW MAY I KNOW IT?

ONE hardly need describe, to an ordinarily intelligent mind, how he may know that he is saved to the uttermost. *He will know it.* As Dr. Daniel Steele very properly says: "You will not need to light a candle to see the sun rise."

1. *You will know it, because the Spirit of God will tell you.*

Do you inquire, in what that witness consists? It is an inward impression on the soul, whereby the Spirit of God immediately and directly witnesses to my spirit that all my sins are removed, and that I am filled with love. It does not differ in manner from the witness to our justification, so much as to the thing

witnessed to. This witness cannot be coun-
terfeited. It will be known. You do not
hear a voice, nor see a form, nor feel a touch;
but there comes to your consciousness — to
your spirit — such an assurance — that you
cannot mistake it.

2. *Deliverance from doubt, is an evidence of
heart purity.*

To be able to say with Faber,

"I know not what it is to doubt,"

is to be far beyond ordinary Christian experience. "Lord, increase our faith," is the
almost constant cry of the average believer.
He often doubts his own acceptance, and fails
to believe the promises. Indeed, he is ever
inquiring, "Is this promise to be taken in its
broadest sense? Is there not some qualifica-
tion to be made? It seems too good to be
true."

But when one enters the valley of blessing — the blessing of heart purity — doubt
no longer throws a mist over the soul. The

very element of doubt is removed, and the soul "staggers not at the promise of God," but is "strong in faith, giving glory to God." "Perfect consecration," says Dr. Steele, "is the doorway out of the most inveterate unbelief. This is also the perfect cure for doubt."

"In Bunyan's immortal allegory there is a scene which strikingly portrays unbelief, doubt, and faith. Christian and Pliable tumble together into the Slough of Despond. Pliable wallows till he gets out 'on that side of the slough which is next to his own house; so away he went, and Christian saw him no more.' This is living on the wrong side of doubt, and going into the darkness of confirmed unbelief. Christian 'struggled to that side of the slough which was fartherest from his own house, and next to the wicket gate.' He lived on the right side of doubt, and reached the Celestial City, while Pliable perished in the City of Destruction. Christian did nobly, but he might have done much better. There was another pilgrim, named Faithful, who, on coming to the same slough, looked carefully, and found 'substantial steps placed, even through the very midst of this slough,' and walked in safety upon them. These steps are the Divine promises, and this character, Faithful, represents all perfect believers in Christ Jesus, lifted by faith above the quagmire while planting their feet upon the immutable granite of God's Word." — *Love Enthroned*, pp. 211, 212.

The pure in heart are properly *believers*, not doubters, and "believing, they rejoice with joy unspeakable and full of glory." Theirs is a chronic faith — not evanescent — not spasmodic — but abiding — a full assurance of faith. And in this particular their faith is distinguished from that found in lower states of experience.

3. *Victory over sin, without long-continued and painful struggle.*

If victory comes to the regenerate soul, it is generally at the end of a long-continued and desperate struggle. The battle is hard fought, and defeat is too often the result. Charles Wesley has well described this conflict: —

> " When, O my Saviour, shall it be
>   That I no more shall break with Thee ?
>   When shall this war of passion cease,
>   And I enjoy a lasting peace ?
>
>   Now I repent; now sin again;
>   Now I revive; and now am slain;
>   Slain with the same malignant dart,
>   Which, O! too often wounds Thy heart.
>
>   When, gracious Lord, when shall it be
>   That I shall find my all in Thee, —
>   The fulness of Thy promise prove,
>   And feast on Thine eternal love ? "

To a purified heart, the conflict may be sharp at times, but it is brief. Satan comes, as he came to Jesus, but finding nothing in us — no property to which he can lay claim — no contraband goods on board — he fires a broadside and retires. There are no enemies within to plot our ruin, or betray us into the hands of our foe. Indeed, the whole soul is friendly to God. It is not divided in its at-

tachments. It can concentrate all its forces
to resist an attack from the foe, and is not
obliged, at the same time, to detail one-half
of its available force to keep in subjection
disloyalty in the citadel. Mr. A says: "I
feel *free* — I have no weights upon my soul.
I have no evil desires clamoring for gratifica-
tion." Mr. B says: "I feel *clean* — I am
washed — I'm made pure. O the luxury of
being clean! There is nothing so sweet as
being 'washed in the blood of the Lamb.'"
Mr. C says: "I am full of *love* — I love every-
body and everything which God has made.
I love beasts and birds and all nature, and es-
pecially the souls of men." He sings, with
Faber: —

> "I love Thee so, I know not how
> My transports to control,
> Thy love is like a burning fire
> Within my very soul."

He cries out, with John Wesley: —

> "O love, thou bottomless abyss,
> My sins are swallowed up in thee! '

4. *There is an insatiable desire kindled in the soul, to tell others of the bliss, and help them to its possession.*

This feeling is well expressed by David Brainerd. "I long," he says, "to be a flame of fire continually glowing in the Divine service, preaching and building up Christ's kingdom to my latest, my dying hour." The justified soul feels this, but it is often dampened by doubt, and chilled by the spiritual death which prevails around. It surrenders to custom, and worldly policy, and is too often hushed entirely. But in the sanctified soul it "becomes a passion, inflaming all the soul like a mighty furnace." They must tell it. The world and a cold church say, it is a *one idea* with them. They are narrow in their views — can see only one thing. This is true, properly understood. They have but *one idea*, but that idea is an *uttermost salvation*. If it is *narrow*, it extends to the outer limits of human need. It is true, they see only one thing; but it is like losing sight of all the stars, when the sun is pouring his full-orbed light upon us. " It implies such a large manifestation of the Divine presence and love," says Mr. Wesley, "that the former in justification, is as nothing in comparison to it." So hot is the fire within, and so anxious are they that others should experience the blessing, that they urge, entreat, and earnestly plead with them to come and be fully saved. This testimony and earnest appeal is not relished by backslidden church members, nor by those who seem content to plod on in the " O wretched man that I am " way.

Dear reader, let us urge you to accept the doctrine of an uttermost salvation, as set forth in this little work, based, as it is, on the unerring word of God, and follow the simple, and, as it seems to us, plain directions here given, and you shall prove that " the blood of Jesus Christ cleanseth from all sin." You shall be lifted into a higher and more satisfactory experience than you have yet known; such an experience as shall make you more happy in your soul, more uniform in your life, and more useful in your labors.

CHAPTER V.

THE ESTABLISHMENT OF BELIEVERS IN HOLINESS.

To have the heart established in "unblamable holiness before God" (1 Thess. iii. 13), so that it will not oscillate, or vibrate, but retain its position and relations, is a blessing of incalculable value. To be saved from all sin is one thing — to retain that experience without backsliding, is another.

There is an appalling amount of instability in the Church of God. Few, comparatively, retain their justification. The same is true in relation to entire sanctification, only not to the same extent. Mr. Wesley said, that very few retained the perfect love of God, or became established in holiness, without losing the experience several times. A minister —

a doctor of divinity — once said, in the presence of several ministers: "I have sought, found, and lost, the blessing of entire sanctification, at least fifty times." In all parts of the land, hundreds of ministers and thousands of members have professed this grace, who now deny it, or make no pretensions to its enjoyment. There are others who are classed with those who believe in and profess the experience, but they are seldom heard from. They believe in the doctrine, and when assailed, defend it. They get blessed at camp-meetings, but failing to become established, they are soon silent. They do not feel clear to confess they do not enjoy the blessing, and yet it is a strain upon the conscience to confess they have it; consequently they remain silent, and soon die.

The Causes of such Instability.

A discovery of the *cause*, may help us in a discovery of the *remedy*.

1. *Want of a definite experience is a fruitful cause of instability.*

There is no substitute for a clear experience of heart purity. Defective instruction, or good counsel neglected, lead to a defective experience. When you hear a professor of entire sanctification say, " I profess the blessing, but have not the witness"; or, "I love God with all my heart, but am not satisfied"; you may be assured that there is a defect somewhere. While it is true that we are saved by faith, our faith, be it remembered, may not grasp the blessing fully. There must be a complete devotement of all to God, followed by an unshaken faith in the blood that cleanseth us, and a steady faith for the direct witness of the Spirit. No one should consider the work complete without the witness of the Spirit. A clear, positive experience, is an indispensable aid to stability.

2. *Sight, or sense-walking, is another cause of instability.*

"We walk by faith, not by sight," is an important apostolic announcement. To walk by sight is to walk by *sense*. To walk by *sense* is to walk by *feeling*. It is to measure our piety by our feelings. When our emotions run high, we judge we are well supplied by grace; but in the absence of emotion, we conclude we are destitute of grace. This state of things will greatly cripple us in our religious life.

Feeling, however, is not to be ignored in religion. A religion without feeling is formalism, and a religion of little else than feeling is fanaticism. But a religion of *faith*, working by love, imparts spiritual life to formalism, and gives steadiness and common sense to fanaticism. Feelings can never be uniform. They are affected by natural temperament, education, and health. If we are governed by our feelings we shall be unstable.

The religion of Christ is a religion of faith, and a religion of faith knows no change.

Faith rests upon the promises, and they are "yea and amen in Christ Jesus." Many professed Christians are like sail-craft, whose direction and speed are dependent on the direction in which the wind blows. If the wind is fair, they make speed; but if head winds come, they are ready to sing —

"In vain we tune our formal songs,
   In vain we strive to rise;
Hosannas languish on our tongues,
   And our devotion dies."

When we attain to that experience described by the apostle — "That Christ may *abide* in your hearts by faith" — we shall have reached heart stability.

3. *A failure to frankly confess the grace which God has given, is sure to result in insta-bility and loss.*

A very large proportion of those who have lost the blessing of heart purity, did so by failing to humbly confess what God had done for them. Experience ought to teach us lessons of wisdom here. We are often exhorted not to make confession of the possession of this grace. We listen to the instruction and soon have occasion to confess that we no longer have the blessing to confess. Those who retain perfect love confess it. We do not ignore *faith* as the condition of receiving and retaining perfect love, but we mean to say that such is the relation of confession to faith, that the one cannot long exist where the other is neglected.

The reasons for this neglect are many and plausible. (1) We do not wish to offend, but rather to win the people. But we do offend by this neglect to tell what Jesus has done for us. We offend God, and Jesus whom He has sent. We grieve the Holy Ghost, by whose power we are wholly sanctified.

(2) We wish to avoid being singular. We are fearful that we shall turn people away from us, and the truth. But such a course does not help the cause. A refusal to testify for Christ makes holiness no less distasteful

to worldly professors. Theirs is a heart-trouble, which only grace can remove. Holiness was designed to make us a " peculiar people," and we seriously compromise our faith by our silence. If we wish to avoid unfavorable criticism, we can do so, but we do so at the expense of the enjoyment of perfect love.

4. *Inactivity is a fruitful cause of instability.*

There is no saving faith which does not work by love, for "faith without works is dead." Some conclude that perfect rest is cessation from labor. But perfect rest means hands and head and heart full of earnest toil. Entire deliverance from inbred sin means more than personal introspection and singing psalm-tunes. It does this, but it means more; it is in labors more abundant.

5. *Opposition is a cause of instability.*

Talk of it as we will, complain of it as we may, it is nevertheless true, that the most depressing and withering opposition to holiness

comes from persons in the church. If it were
an enemy, then could we more easily endure
it. But it is from those with whom we go to
the house of God in company. After a poor
soul, who has been burdened beyond measure,
arises in their place in the prayer or confer-
ence meeting and tells, in earnest words, of
the bliss which has come to their hearts, and
that the blood of Jesus Christ has cleansed
them from all sin, — to have the pastor of that
soul arise and say, " If people would only *live*
their religion and not say so much about
it, they would show much more wisdom,"
or, " We have not much faith in those high
professions; we want to see people *live* their
religion," — such a reply is a little crushing
to an ordinarily sensitive soul. In a thousand
ways, — in inuendoes and slurs against holiness and its professors, in prayer-meeting
talks and Sabbath sermons, — these people
who are trying to follow the Lord with a pure
heart, are crossed and reproved and censured
and criticised. After a time they cease to be

heard, they fall into darkness, and the light goes out.

These are a few of the causes of instability. Many more might be named.

The Cure of Instability.

Remove the cause. Remedy the evils named and the life will become uniform, and we shall have stable professors of holiness.

1. Be sure that your experience is clear and satisfactory. There is no substitute for this. Some persons ignore the direct witness of the Spirit. They insist that the *Word* is sufficient for them. Listen not to such for a moment. You are entitled to a direct witness of the Spirit. God has promised it, and it shall be given to you.

2. Let your walk be one of faith more than of feeling. Remember that all the promises are for you, and they are all "yea and amen in Christ Jesus." If you follow your feelings you will not have much; but if you walk by faith you will have all the feeling you need.

He who pays least attention to his feelings, generally has most enjoyment.

3. Do not fail to confess all that God has done for you. A failure here is perilous. The soul withers and dies when it ceases to glorify God as a witness. On this reef many have foundered.

4. Be full of good works. Faith without works will soon die. God says, "Work"; not as a *condition* of salvation, but as a condition of *reward*. Man is saved by faith, but rewarded according to his works. No man ever became established in holiness who did not do, in some way, a good deal of hard work at soul-saving and body-blessing.

5. Cultivate a loving spirit, and "the Lord will make you to abound more and more."

We need not enlarge on these points — they should be sufficiently clear to all. "Stand fast in the liberty wherewith Christ hath made you free, and be not entangled again with the yoke of bondage."

Then let us sing, with the Spirit and with the understanding : —

> " Jesus, plant and root in me
> All the mind that was in Thee;
> Settled peace I then shall find;
> Jesus' is a quiet mind.
>
> Anger I no more shall feel, —
> Always even, always still, —
> Meekly on my God reclined, —
> Jesus' is a gentle mind.
>
> I shall suffer and fulfil
> All my Father's gracious will;
> Be in all alike resigned;
> Jesus' is a patient mind.
>
> Lowly, loving, meek, and pure,
> I shall to the end endure;
> Be no more to sin inclined;
> Jesus' is a constant mind."

Holiness Books.

New Testament Standard of Piety.
By Rev. W. McDonald. With a steel portrait of the author. Price 50 cts.

Scriptural Way of Holiness.
By Rev. W. McDonald. Price 75 cts.

Marquis De Renty.
By Rev. W. McDonald. Price 60 cts.

God's Method with Man.
By Rev. B. W. Gorham. Price $1.00

Offices of the Holy Spirit.
By Dougan Clark, M.D. Price 75 cts.

The Historical Position of Wesleyan Methodism on the Subject of Holiness.
(Just issued.) By Rev. Chas. Munger. Price 10 cts.

The Second Blessing Demonstrated.
(Just issued.) By Rev. B. F. Gassaway. Price 10 cts.

Inheritance Restored.
By Rev. M. L. Haney. Price $1.00.

Love Enthroned.
By Daniel Steele, D.D. Price $1.25.

Milestone Papers.
By Daniel Steele, D.D. Price 85 cts.

Holiness Bible Readings.
By Rev. Isaiah Reid. Price 60 cts.

McDONALD & GILL,
36 BROMFIELD ST. - - - - BOSTON.